Butterfly

Meadow

Dazzle's
New Friend

Come flutter by

Butterfly
Meadow!

and the next Butterfly Meadow
adventure . . .

Butterfly Meadow

Dazzle's New Friend

by Olivia Moss
illustrated by Helen Turner

SCHOLASTIC INC.

New York Toronto London Auckland Sydney
Mexico City New Delhi Hong Kong Buenos Aires

With special thanks to Narinder Dhami

For Courtney Mitchell — a true friend

No part of this publication may be reproduced, stored in a retrieval system, or transmitted in any form or by any means, electronic, mechanical, photocopying, recording, or otherwise, without written permission of the publisher. For information regarding permission, write to Working Partners Limited, Stanley House, St. Chad's Place, London WC1X 9HH, United Kingdom.

ISBN-13: 978-0-545-05460-7
ISBN-10: 0-545-05460-5

12 11 10 9 8 7 6 5 4 3 2 1   8 9 10 11 12 13/0

Printed in the U.S.A.

First printing, December 2008

Contents

CHAPTER ONE

Fun in the Orchard

"Ready?" Dazzle called excitedly, fluttering her pale yellow wings. "Here we go!"

Dazzle and her butterfly friends, Skipper, Twinkle, and Mallow, were playing in the apple orchard. They'd found a big fallen leaf balanced on the branch of an apple tree and were using it

as a seesaw. Dazzle and Twinkle perched
on one side of the leaf, with Skipper and
Mallow on the other side. They rocked
as fast as they could.

Dazzle loved seeing how the bright
sunshine filtered through the leaves and
made her friends' wings glow. On such a
beautiful day, Dazzle didn't have a care
in the world!

"Let's bounce even higher, Dazzle,"
Twinkle suggested.

The two butterflies flew up into the
air, then dove down onto the leaf.
The leaf tipped and sent Mallow and
Skipper sailing up toward the sky.

"Yay!" Skipper laughed, swooping
back down. "This is so much fun!"

"Now it's our turn," Twinkle said
eagerly.

3

This time, Skipper and Mallow flew up high, then dove down on their side of the leaf. Dazzle and Twinkle soared into the air.

"Wheee!" the two butterflies cried, giggling.

Dazzle couldn't wait to do it again! She was so lucky to have friends like Skipper, Mallow, and Twinkle to play with in the orchard near Butterfly Meadow.

"It's our turn now," Mallow called. But as Dazzle and Twinkle landed on the other side of the leaf, a gruff voice rang through the air.

"Excuse me!"

The four butterflies froze and looked at one another in surprise.

"Who said that?" asked Skipper, looking around the apple tree.

"I did!" the voice replied.

"It's coming from down there," said Dazzle, pointing to the ground.

The butterflies all peered through the leaves. Near the bottom of the tree

trunk, they saw two spiky hedgehogs sniffing around in the grass.

"Have you seen any hedgehogs around the orchard today?" the biggest one called.

"Only you two," Twinkle said, grinning.

The hedgehogs glanced at each other. The smaller hedgehog shook its head slowly.

"What's wrong?" asked Dazzle, as she and her friends flew down to the ground.

"We can't find our son, Prickle, anywhere," the father hedgehog said, looking through the clumps of grass at the bottom of the tree. "We were hoping you might have seen him."

"Prickle's not even supposed to *be* in the orchard," the mother hedgehog explained. "But he loves to explore, so sometimes he forgets the rules."

"Oh, no!" Dazzle couldn't help feeling worried. She perched on a yellow daisy near the hedgehogs. Then she glanced at Mallow, Twinkle, and Skipper. "Why don't we fly around the orchard and look for Prickle?" she suggested. "We can cover much more ground than the hedgehogs can!"

"That's a great idea!" agreed Mallow, twirling excitedly.

"Let's get started," Twinkle added.

"Oh, thank you all," the father hedgehog said. "You're not just beautiful, you're very kind, too!"

"I am awfully pretty, aren't I?" Twinkle agreed happily, bobbing in the air.

7

Dazzle tried not to smile. Twinkle was
a peacock butterfly. She was very proud
of the beautiful colors and patterns on
her wings.

"What does Prickle look like?" asked
Mallow. "We'll need to be able to
recognize him when we see him."

"Well, he looks like us," the father
hedgehog replied. "Lots of needles on his
back, small black eyes — that kind of
thing. He's just smaller."

"We'll do our best to find him,"
Skipper vowed.

"We'll head home to look after our
other children," the mother hedgehog
said, looking relieved. "Please let us
know right away if you find Prickle!"

"Yes, of course," Dazzle promised.

"Thank you!" the hedgehogs cried.
They scuttled off through the grass, their
prickly spines moving from side to side.

"Come on," called Twinkle, batting
her red-and-blue wings. "Let's find
Prickle!"

CHAPTER TWO

That's No Hedgehog!

Dazzle and her friends zigzagged their way between the apple trees. They flew close to the ground so that they could see Prickle if he was nearby. They spotted squirrels scampering up and down tree trunks, bees busy collecting nectar, and spiders spinning webs between the flower

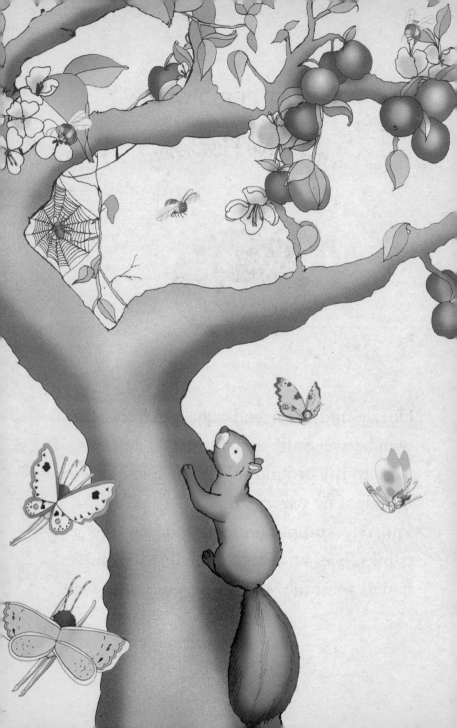

stalks. But there was no sign of a hedgehog anywhere.

Suddenly, Twinkle shouted, "Oh! I can see something moving around in one of those bushes!"

She swooped down toward the bush. Mallow had flown ahead, but Dazzle and Skipper followed Twinkle. Dazzle hoped that they had found Prickle! The little hedgehog would probably be feeling lonely by now. Dazzle remembered how lost she'd felt on her first day in Butterfly Meadow, before she had made friends.

"Hello?" Twinkle called, flying up to the bush. "Is that Prickle? Please come out, whoever you are!"

The leaves rustled. Dazzle held her breath, hoping to see the prickly spines of a hedgehog. But instead, a furry brown creature with floppy ears popped its head out of the bush. It was a rabbit!

"Oh!" said Skipper. "Sorry to bother you. We thought you might be the hedgehog we're looking for."

The rabbit twitched its nose. "No. Sorry about that!" he replied, hopping back into the bush.

Just then, the three butterflies heard Mallow calling them from up ahead. "Dazzle! Twinkle! Skipper! Over here!"

"It sounds like Mallow found something," Dazzle said breathlessly. She darted away as fast as she could, with Skipper and Twinkle close behind.

CHAPTER THREE

Follow the Apples!

Mallow was bobbing in the air nearby, waiting for her friends. "Look!" she said, tipping her wing toward the ground.

Dazzle, Skipper, and Twinkle glanced down and saw an apple core lying on the grass.

"Someone's been eating apples,"

Mallow went on. "I wonder who it could be?"

"There's another half-eaten apple over there," said Dazzle, pointing up ahead with her wing.

The group of butterflies fluttered over to the next apple core and looked around.

"And there's another one!" Twinkle cried. "It's a whole trail of half-eaten apples!"

"Let's follow it," Skipper suggested. "Maybe it will lead us to Prickle."

The butterflies flew over the trail of apple cores, winding in and out of the trees.

"There are lots of apples on the ground," Mallow remarked. "And they all look like someone's been munching on them."

"I'd have a stomachache if I ate that much," Skipper added. Then she paused

in mid-air,
fluttering her
wings silently.
"I can hear
something."

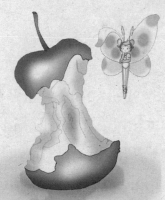

The other
butterflies stopped,
listening carefully.

"I hear something,
too," Dazzle whispered.

Mallow flew closer to the sound.
"Look. Over here!" The four
butterflies swooped down toward the
ground.

A strange creature sat on the grass,
munching on an apple. It was eating
with loud slurps. Dazzle realized that
was the noise she had heard. The
creature had a long snout and spines just

like a hedgehog, but it also had bits of apple stuck all over its face — and a big bump growing out of its back!

"What is that?" Dazzle asked her friends.

"Let's look closer," Twinkle suggested quietly.

The butterflies dipped toward the ground. As they did, the strange

creature suddenly glanced up and spotted them.

"What are you staring at?" it asked in a squeaky voice. Its mouth was full of apple and little pieces flew everywhere. Mallow even had to dodge out of the way to avoid being hit by one of them!

Dazzle didn't mean to stare, but she'd *never* seen anything like this animal before in her life.

CHAPTER FOUR

Prickle in a Pickle

"We're sorry for staring," Skipper said politely, hovering in the air. "But we were wondering what kind of animal you are."

The creature glared at her. "I'm a hedgehog, of course!" he said. "Haven't you ever seen a hedgehog before?"

"I've never seen a hedgehog with a big

bump on its back like you have," Dazzle told him. Could this be Prickle? His mom and dad hadn't said anything about the big bump on his back.

"What are you talking about?" the hedgehog spluttered, looking embarrassed. "I don't have a bump on my back!"

"Well, we're not making it up," Mallow said gently to the hedgehog. "Why don't you look for yourself?"

The hedgehog sighed. He dropped the apple core he was munching and twisted around to look at his back. Then he twisted the other way. Soon he was going around and around in circles, but he still couldn't see his own back. Dazzle and the other butterflies tried not to laugh.

"Well!" The hedgehog's spines were bristling with annoyance. "I think all you butterflies must be seeing things. There's nothing wrong with me!"

"How can he *not* know he has something growing out of his back?" Twinkle whispered. Dazzle shrugged. She couldn't understand why the hedgehog kept insisting that nothing was wrong!

While the butterflies bobbed up and down in the air, Twinkle frowned. She lifted her head and sniffed.

"Do you smell that?" she asked.

Twinkle allowed the breeze to blow her from one spot to another as she followed the smell. Then she flew closer to the ground, until she was right above the hedgehog's bump.

Dazzle followed Twinkle. Now she noticed the smell, too! It was sweet and sharp all at the same time. Dazzle and Twinkle peered at the large, mushy bump on the hedgehog's back.

"Oh, now I see what it is," Twinkle cried. "It's a rotten apple. It must be stuck on his spines!"

The hedgehog looked sheepish.

"Um, well, yes," he said in his squeaky voice. "I thought I could feel something on my back. I mean, I knew it was there all along."

"You knew?" Mallow stared at him in surprise. "Then why did you pretend that there was nothing on your back?"

"I was just testing you," the hedgehog mumbled, shuffling his feet.

Dazzle didn't believe him. She huddled close to her butterfly friends. "I don't think he wants to admit that he needs our help," she whispered.

"I wonder how the apple got stuck on his back in the first place?"

Skipper said, forgetting to keep her voice down.

"Well, if you must know," the hedgehog squeaked, "I was taking a nap. Eating apples can be hard work! I felt a thump and woke up. But I thought I'd dreamed it."

"It must have been the apple falling from the tree — and landing on top of you," said Mallow. She flew around the hedgehog, inspecting him carefully. "At least you're not hurt."

"Don't worry," Dazzle said kindly. "We'll help you get the apple off. We can't get too close to your prickly spines, since they could tear our wings. But I'm sure we'll think of something!"

"No," the hedgehog replied quickly. "I don't need any help! I'm fine, thank you.

I'm just going to finish my nap now. Good-bye." He squeezed his eyes tightly shut.

"He's only pretending to go to sleep, I bet," Mallow said in a low voice. The hedgehog began to snore loudly. "He can't be comfortable with an apple stuck on his back like that!"

"He won't be able to walk properly, either," Skipper pointed out. "That apple looks heavy."

"What should we do?" asked Twinkle. "We can't just leave him like this!"

CHAPTER FIVE

Upside Down

Dazzle watched as Skipper flew over to the hedgehog and landed on his nose.

"Do you mind?" the hedgehog grumbled, opening his eyes. His spines bristled.

"You could be a little nicer to us," Skipper pointed out, balancing on the

hedgehog's nose. "We're only trying
to help."

"Why do you want to help me?" the
hedgehog asked.

"We've spent all this time looking
for you," Mallow said, nodding
knowingly at the hedgehog from the air
above. "We're not going to abandon
you now."

"Looking for me? Why?" the hedgehog glanced at Dazzle and each of her friends in turn.

"Isn't your name Prickle?" asked Skipper.

"How do you know that?" As the hedgehog spoke, he reached out to grab one of the nearby apples on the ground. Dazzle had to swoop between him and the apple to keep him from trying to take a bite. *No more apples for you!* she thought, grinning.

"Your mom and dad are worried about you," Skipper explained.

"And we said we'd help find you," Dazzle added.

"You really should go home right away," Mallow chimed in.

Prickle stared at his feet. "I *do* want to go home," he admitted at last. His tummy gave a loud growl. "I'm not even supposed to be in the orchard. But I can't get home with this apple on my back. It's too hard to walk. Please, will you help me?"

"Of course we'll help you, Prickle," Dazzle piped up, flying a loop in the air in excitement. "We just have to

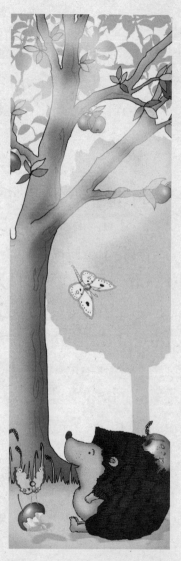

figure out how." She glanced at the other butterflies. "Any ideas?"

"Look how rough the bark of this apple tree is," Twinkle said suddenly. "Maybe Prickle could use the tree trunk to scratch the apple off his spines."

"That's a great idea, Twinkle!" Dazzle agreed. "Prickle, do you think you can walk over to the tree?"

Prickle sighed as his tummy growled again. "I'll try," he replied.

The butterflies flew around Prickle as he took one step forward, then another. Dazzle could see that the apple on the hedgehog's back was heavy. It made him sway from side to side.

"My tummy hurts!" Prickle groaned as he took another unsteady step. "I think I ate too many apples."

"Not far to go now, Prickle," Skipper said. She flew backward, leading Prickle along. "Come on, just a few more steps toward me."

Suddenly, Prickle tripped over a piece of apple lying in the grass and lost his balance. Dazzle gasped as the hedgehog toppled onto his side. Prickle tried desperately to roll himself back onto his paws. He almost managed to get right side up, but it was no use. He rolled onto his back. His four little paws waved helplessly in the air.

"Oh, no!" Twinkle cried, zooming down toward him. "Can you turn over again, Prickle?"

"No!" the hedgehog squeaked. "I can't move!"

"And look, the apple's really stuck on his spines now," Dazzle pointed out. "This is a disaster!"

Dazzle felt terrible. She and her friends had been trying to help, and now they'd made things worse.

"Let's see if we can push Prickle back over," she suggested to the others.

The four butterflies took hold of Prickle's little paws and tried to rock him upright. Dazzle leaned against one of Prickle's feet, but her wings got in the way. She could see that Prickle was hardly moving at all. The hedgehog was just too heavy for them.

"Ooh!" Prickle groaned, stranded on his back. "I feel *really* ill now. My tummy hurts!"

"We need to get him on his feet, and fast!" Mallow cried.

CHAPTER SIX

Let's Tickle Prickle!

"I have an idea! I think I know how we can help Prickle get back on his feet," Dazzle said.

"How?" Twinkle asked. "He's much too heavy for us to lift!"

"And we can't get too close to his prickly spines," Skipper added, looking nervous.

Dazzle lowered her voice so that Prickle couldn't hear. "If we all take turns tickling Prickle with our wings, maybe he'll laugh so much that he'll rock back onto his feet!"

Dazzle's friends smiled mischievously. "Sounds like fun," Skipper said.

Mallow and Twinkle darted over to Prickle again. Mallow landed on one of Prickle's back paws, and Twinkle fluttered down onto the other. Then, as Dazzle and Skipper watched, the two butterflies began to lightly tickle the hedgehog's paws with their wings.

"What are you doing?" Prickle yelped. "Ha, ha, ha! Stop! It tickles! Hee, hee!"

Skipper and Dazzle flew over to Prickle and landed lightly on his nose.

"Your tiny butterfly feet are tickling me!" the hedgehog giggled, making Dazzle and Skipper laugh, too.

Prickle began to squirm. Dazzle watched hopefully as he rocked back and forth, rolling with laughter. Would the hedgehog be able to get back on his feet?

"Oh, I'm going to sneeze!" Prickle said suddenly.

Quickly, the butterflies flew out of the way.

"*A-a-a-a-choo*!" Prickle gave a huge sneeze. He rocked forward sharply, and Dazzle's wings trembled with excitement.

But even though Prickle's paws grazed the grass, the

force of the sneeze wasn't enough to get him right side up. He rolled onto his back again and looked up at the butterflies in the sky above him.

"Please don't do that again!" Prickle said, sighing. "I don't think I can take much more tickling!"

"So what should we do *now*?" Mallow asked her friends.

Dazzle thought hard. She was determined not to leave Prickle stuck in the orchard. There *had* to be a way to get the hedgehog back on his feet.

"Do you remember when we were bouncing on the seesaw leaf this morning?" Dazzle said slowly, still working out an idea in her head. "Maybe we can make a seesaw for Prickle."

"That's perfect, Dazzle!" said Mallow.

"You mean we're going to send
Prickle shooting through the air?"
Twinkle asked. "I've never seen a flying
hedgehog before!"

"Hedgehogs can't fly!" Prickle called
out, looking worried. "We like to stay on
the ground."

"It's a great idea," said Skipper. "But
how are we going to make it work?
We're not strong enough to bounce

Prickle up into the air ourselves. And what if he hurts himself when he lands?"

"We need a safety net to catch Prickle," Dazzle replied. She used her wing to point at two spiders that were spinning large, glittering webs in a nearby bush. "I thought we could ask the spiders to weave us a web between those two apple trees."

"Good thinking, Dazzle!" Twinkle said, nodding her head. "And remember the squirrels we saw earlier?" Dazzle went on. "They could help us make a seesaw from a tree branch.

The squirrels are much heavier than we are, so *they* could be the ones that jump onto the other side of the seesaw and send Prickle flying."

Prickle had been listening to all this, and he looked *very* nervous.

"Do you really think this is going to work?" he called. Dazzle could understand why he was worried, but she and her friends would do whatever it took to get Prickle back to his mom and dad.

"We have to *try*," Dazzle said. "It's our only chance."

CHAPTER SEVEN

Can Hedgehogs Fly?

"Twinkle, you and Mallow go and round up the spiders," Dazzle instructed. "Skipper and I will find the squirrels."

Dazzle realized how much more confident she was now than when she'd first emerged from her cocoon as a shy young butterfly. *I hope my plan works,* she thought.

Twinkle and Mallow darted off, while Dazzle and Skipper flew up into the trees.

"Don't worry, Prickle," Skipper called back. "We'll have you on your feet in no time."

Dazzle and Skipper wove between the tree branches. After a moment, they spotted two squirrels near the top of a tree. The squirrels were chattering excitedly as they hid a pile of nuts inside a hole in the trunk.

"Hello," Dazzle called.

"Ooh, butterflies!" the smaller squirrel exclaimed. "You're so pretty!"

"Thank you," Dazzle replied. "We were wondering if you could help us." She explained what had happened to

Prickle and told the squirrels about her seesaw idea.

"Oh, the poor hedgehog!" the smaller squirrel said. "Of course, we'll help. Let's go right away!"

The two squirrels scampered down the tree trunk, their bushy tails waving. Dazzle and Skipper flew after them. Before long, the squirrels arrived at the bottom of the tree and hopped excitedly around a fallen branch.

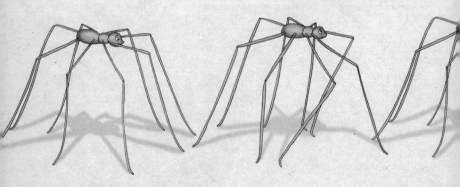

"Look, we found the perfect seesaw!"
one of the squirrels called to Dazzle and
Skipper.

"Nice job!" Dazzle said gratefully.

"Here come Mallow and Twinkle."
Skipper pointed a wing at their friends,
who were flying back through the trees
toward them. "And look, Dazzle!
They've gathered up a whole army of
spiders."

Dazzle saw a long line of spiders

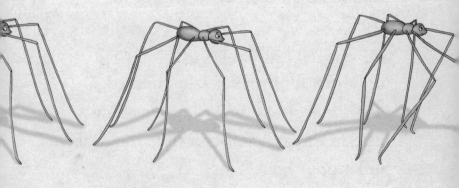

walking through the grass on spindly legs. "Thanks, Mallow and Twinkle!" she called. "And thank you, spiders, for coming to help."

The spiders all stopped, and the one at the front of the line stared at poor Prickle.

"Hmm," it said. "We're going to need an extra-strong net." It turned to the other spiders. "Let's get spinning, guys!"

The spiders began to spin a sturdy net between two of the trees. The squirrels dragged the fallen branch over to Prickle.

"One end of the branch has to go underneath him," Dazzle directed. "Prickle, could you rock yourself just a little so the squirrels can slide the branch under your back?"

"I hope this works," Prickle said with a sigh as he rolled to one side. "Otherwise, I'm going to be here forever!"

"Try to think positive, Prickle!" Mallow cheered.

But Dazzle had noticed that Prickle's spines were trembling. She flew over to him.

"Are you all right, Prickle?" she asked softly.

"I'm *afraid* to fly," he admitted.

"Flying's so much fun," Dazzle assured him.

"Yes — if you have wings!" Prickle muttered, looking unhappy.

"Look, the spiders have spun a really strong net to catch you." Dazzle pointed her wing at the enormous, glistening cobweb. "All you have to do is trust us. We're your friends."

The two squirrels scampered back up the tree and positioned themselves over one end of the seesaw. Then the spiders crawled to the edges of the net, safely out of the way.

Mallow, Twinkle, and Skipper hovered nearby, watching anxiously.

"Ready?" Dazzle asked their hedgehog friend. "Can you trust us?"

Prickle hesitated, then gave a firm nod of his head. Dazzle felt herself flush with happiness — he was going to do it! She just knew this was going to work.

"Close your eyes and get ready, Prickle!" Dazzle said.

"I'm ready," Prickle whispered, his voice shaking.

Dazzle looked up at the squirrels. "One, two, three, GO!" she cried.

The two squirrels launched themselves out of the tree and soared through the air.

"Wheee!" they both cried out.
They landed with a thump on one
end of the seesaw. Prickle shot up into
the air.

He was flying!

CHAPTER EIGHT

Back Home

Dazzle watched as Prickle zoomed
through the air toward the spiders' net.

"Here I come!" Prickle shouted.

Everyone watched as the hedgehog
landed right in the center of the cobweb.
He bounced a few times, but the net
didn't break.

"Let's hear it for Prickle!" the biggest spider yelled. "Hip, hip, hooray!"

Everyone cheered.

"Prickle, you did it!" Dazzle cried, fluttering over to the cobweb. "You're the bravest hedgehog *ever*!"

"I was very scared," Prickle admitted, "but it was fun!"

The spiders rushed forward to help him get down, and he rolled carefully out of the net. The apple that had been wedged on Prickle's spines was left behind, caught in the fine, sticky threads of the cobweb.

"I'm free!" Prickle cried happily as he reached the ground. He gave himself a shake. "Thank you, spiders. Thank you, squirrels. But most of all, thank you, butterflies!"

Dazzle, Twinkle, Mallow, and Skipper swooped down and peppered Prickle's cheeks with soft butterfly kisses. Prickle blushed, but he also looked pleased.

"I won't forget all my new butterfly friends," he said. "I know I wasn't very nice before, but I'll be a better friend from now on."

"We won't forget you, either, Prickle,"

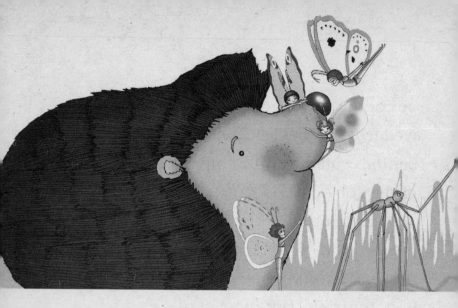

Dazzle replied. "After all, who could
forget a flying hedgehog?"

They all laughed at that, even Prickle.

"It's time for us all to go home,"
said Skipper. She turned to Prickle.
"Your parents will be wondering where
you are."

Prickle's tummy growled loudly.
"I hope they won't expect me to eat
any dinner," he said, looking
queasy again.

Dazzle felt laughter fizzing up inside
of her. "You might not need to eat
anything for a while," she agreed.
"Definitely no more apples!"

"Good-bye," the spiders called as the
four friends and Prickle set off.

"See you later!" shouted the squirrels,
scurrying back up the tree.

The butterflies brought Prickle back
to the place where they'd met his mom
and dad.

"I know my way from here," Prickle said. "Thank you again, for everything."

The sun was beginning to set and the sky was streaked with red. Up ahead, Dazzle could see the long grass and bobbing flowers of Butterfly Meadow. She didn't think she'd ever seen her home looking so beautiful.

"Good-bye!" the butterflies called as Prickle strolled through the grass toward his home. He still swayed from side to side, but now there was no big red apple attached to his spines.

"He looks just like a normal hedgehog again," Mallow commented as the butterflies swooped through the air back to the meadow.

"Except that he isn't a normal

hedgehog. He's a flying hedgehog!"
Dazzle said, laughing. She couldn't wait
to tell all their other butterfly friends
about Prickle. He'd been part of their
best adventure yet!

❀ FUN FACTS! ❀
Meet the Mysterious Hedgehog

You won't find a hedgehog in your backyard. And you won't find one in your playground or in the park. You won't find a single hedgehog roaming free in any of the fifty states. Hedgehogs only live in Europe, Asia, Africa, and New Zealand.

Hedgehogs look like a cross between a mouse and a porcupine. A hedgehog's back is covered with up to 5,000 hollow, yellow-tipped hairs, called spines. A hedgehog might look like a porcupine, but it's much friendlier. Unlike the porcupine, a hedgehog's spines aren't poisonous or barbed. Instead, hedgehogs use their spines to roll into a tight, prickly ball to protect themselves from their enemies.

Hedgehogs usually come out at night. They like to sleep under bushes or rocks when the sun is out. Some hedgehogs also hibernate, sleeping for months when the weather turns cold.

Hedgehogs may be small, but they are noisy! When they're out and about, you might hear a hedgehog before you see one. They grunt, snuffle, and sometimes even squeal.

And wait until you hear what they eat. When they're hungry, hedgehogs can eat insects, snails, frogs, or even slugs. You won't find those on the menu at home!

Dazzle is at home in

Butterfly Meadow!

Here's a sneak peek at her next adventure,

Twinkle and the Busy Bee!

CHAPTER ONE

Mystery in the Meadow

It was a hot, sunny afternoon in
Butterfly Meadow. Dazzle had found a
comfortable spot on a sunflower with
Skipper and Mallow, two of her butterfly
friends. She was just drifting into a
dream about delicious nectar. . . .

"Hey, you guys! Something's wrong
in the meadow."

Dazzle's eyes snapped open. Her friend Twinkle, a colorful peacock butterfly, zipped around the sunflower.

"What's happening?" Dazzle asked. Twinkle was darting around so fast, it made Dazzle's head spin.

Nearby, Mallow fluttered her small white wings. "Is it a mystery?" she asked, flitting into the air. "I love a good mystery!"

Skipper yawned. "Everything looks fine to me," she said, gazing around. "Twinkle, aren't you hot, racing all over the place?"

Twinkle didn't answer. Instead, she zoomed around the sunflower one more time. The bright colors of her wings blurred together as she flew.

"Well?" Dazzle asked. "Aren't you going to tell us what's going on?"

"I'll *show* you," Twinkle replied mysteriously. "Follow me!"

Dazzle stretched out her wings and fluttered toward her friend, with Mallow close behind. "Come on, Skipper," Mallow called back to the holly blue butterfly. "It's not like you to miss out on an adventure."

"Okay, I'm coming," Skipper said, looking sleepy and flapping her pretty blue wings. "Wait up!"

Twinkle led her friends to a thick hedge at the edge of the meadow. She glanced back, then dived down among the leaves. "In here," she called.

Dazzle, Skipper, and Mallow followed

Twinkle, dodging branches. It was cooler out of the sun's glare, but some of the branches had thorns on them. Dazzle fluttered her pale yellow wings carefully.

Just then, Twinkle stopped so suddenly that Dazzle bumped right into her! Skipper skidded into Dazzle, and Mallow tumbled out of the hedge, trying to stop in time.

"Whoa!" Mallow yelped, fluttering her wings to steady herself. "Pileup!"

Dazzle, Twinkle, and Skipper untangled themselves, giggling. "What are we doing in here?" Skipper asked, smoothing her crumpled antennae.

"I'm about to show you," Twinkle replied. She pointed a wing at a cluster of flowers swaying in the grass below the hedge. "There," she said. "See?"

Come flutter by Butterfly Meadow!

Don't miss any of Dazzle's adventures!

There's Magic in Every Book!

The Rainbow Fairies
Books #1-7

The Weather Fairies
Books #1-7

The Jewel Fairies
Books #1-7

The Pet Fairies
Books #1-7

The Fun Day Fairies
Books #1-7

SCHOLASTIC
www.scholastic.com
www.rainbowmagiconline.com

HIT entertainment

FAIRYG